THERE ARE MORNINGS WHEN EVERYTHING IS STILL AND QUIET ALL AROUND YOU. THE LIGHT SHOWS YOU THINGS YOU NEVER SAW BEFORE: LIKE COLORS YOU DIDN'T KNOW WERE THERE UNTIL THEN.

SO IT IS WITH PEOPLE SOMETIMES IN THE LIVES THEY LEAD. WHAT YOU HAVE **BEEN** MAKES YOU WHAT YOU ARE, AND IN HARD TIMES, YOU SEE THINGS IN PEOPLE YOU NEVER SAW BEFORE.

SOMETIMES THE LIGHT SCARCELY MADE ITS WAY INTO POSEY COUNTY. ON THIS DAY IN 1943, WITH THE SLOW EVAPORATION OF DARKNESS, ALL THE COLORS OF MORNING WERE BLEACHED IN A MUTED CONSPIRACY.

WHEN AARON HAYLEY, MY FATHER, DISAPPEARED, IT WAS ONLY APPARENT TO MY BROTHER AND ME. NOBODY ELSE TOOK MUCH NOTICE.

MY MOTHER NEVER TALKED ABOUT IT. SHE TOOK US TO INDIANA IN THE MIDDLE OF THE NIGHT.

IT WASN'T REALLY THAT HE DISAPPEARED-- WE DID. BUT, HE WAS GONE.

I WAS ONLY THREE WHEN WE LEFT OKLAHOMA AND I DIDN'T REALLY FEEL MY FATHER'S ABSENCE. I NOTICED A LACK OF TENSION AS THOUGH SOMEONE HAD SUDDENLY TURNED DOWN A VERY LOUD RADIO.

BUT I DIDN'T REALLY MISS MY FATHER. RAY EDWIN DID. HE REMEMBERED HIM CLEARLY.

WHEN THAT FEELING CAME OVER HIM I KNEW ENOUGH TO LEAVE HIM BE.

MEMORIES FROM THE EARLIEST PART OF MY LIFE ARE FREE FROM DISTRACTION BUT ARE RARELY INCLINED TO STOOP TO FACTS.

IT'S ONLY SEARCHING OLD PHOTOGRAPHS THAT MEMORY GIVES WAY AND I CAN SEE THE INVISIBLE SECRETS: MY MOTHER'S HEAD TURNED IN A SLIGHTLY UNNATURAL WAY; RAY EDWIN'S LONG-SLEEVED SHIRT.

I DON'T REMEMBER ANY BEATINGS. MY BROTHER HAS SAID THAT MY FATHER NEVER RAISED A HAND TO ME.

I REMEMBER A FEW THINGS.

I REMEMBER HIM WINKING AT ME OVER THE TOP OF HIS NEWSPAPER AND I REMEMBER THE SOUR SMELL OF BEER AS HE KISSED ME GOODNIGHT.

SOMETIMES MY FATHER WOULD DRIVE US TO THE CHURCH REVIVAL MEETING ON SUNDAY MORNINGS.

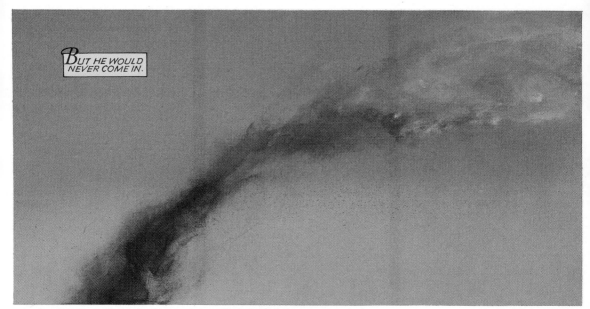

BUT HE WOULD NEVER COME IN.

PLEASE. PLEASE... DON'T KILL ME.

I COULD NOT DO THAT.

YOU'RE SPEAKING ENGLISH!

IS THAT SO? WHO ARE YOU?

I.., AARON HAYLEY USAF. I... I CAN'T FEEL ANYTHING. CAN'T MOVE MY HEAD. IS THIS SOME KIND OF TEMPORARY ARMY HOSPITAL?

THE LAST THING I REMEMBER WE WERE FLYING OVER THE OKINAWA ISLANDS--THE EAST CHINA SEA-- P-38 LIGHTNINGS.

Mmm. I SEE. AARON HAYLEY USAF. YOU WERE FLYING OVER THE OCEAN TO KILL PEOPLE AND THEY SAW YOU FIRST.

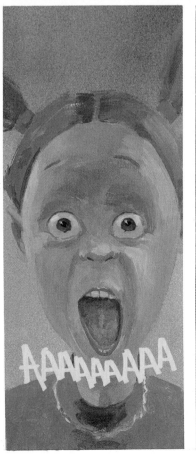

RUSSELL, IF THE PRINCIPAL SENDS YOU HOME AGAIN YOU'RE GOING TO MISS OUR TRIP TO THE FIRE DEPARTMENT.

MERLE, TAKE ANNIE OUT TO THE PUMP AND WASH HER HANDS.

AAAAAA!

AND HELP HER SIMMER DOWN.

WHEN I QUERIED MAMA ABOUT WHAT HAD MADE THE BUTCHIES SO MEAN AND LOATHSOME SHE TOLD ME WHAT THEY LACKED IN THEIR LIVES WAS KINDNESS.

SINCE THEY HAD NOT BEEN SHOWN ANY, THEY HAD NO IDEA HOW TO CULTIVATE IT IN THEM- SELVES.

SHE SAID IF THEY HAD ENOUGH EXPERIENCE WITH CIVILIZATION, THEY WOULD BE ALMOST AS DECENT AS NORMAL PEOPLE.

RAY EDWIN AND I HAD OUR DOUBTS.

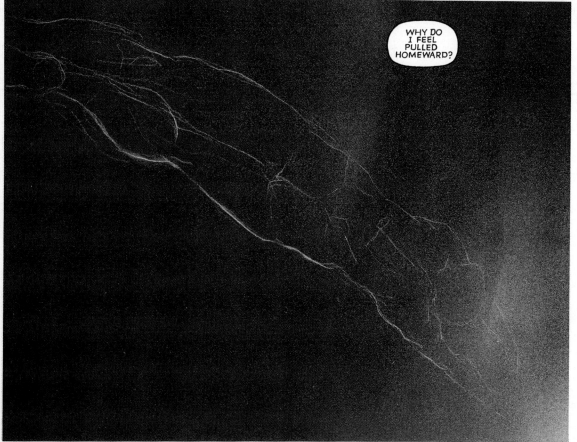

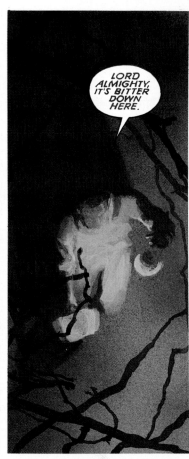

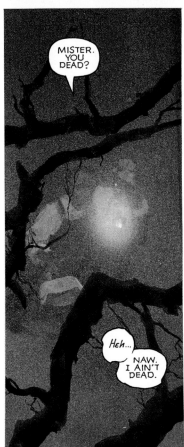

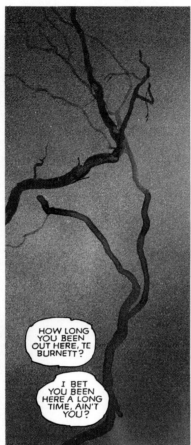

DON'T YOU HAVE ANY PEOPLE? SOMEBODY YOU WANT ME TO CALL ON, FOR YOU?

OH, I GOT ME SOME RELATIVES. I'M SURE THEY'LL BE COMIN' DIRECTLY.

WELL... I RECKON I'LL KEEP WATCH FOR 'EM.

I RECKON YOU WILL.

PERSONALLY, IF I WAS YOU, I'D EAT SOME O' THAT SOUP. WARM YOU UP.

FOUND. A FOUNDLING. LIKE MOSES IN HIS CRADLE, DELIVERED FROM THE RIVER BY THE LAST TO WATCH OVER THIS TREE.

A GYPSY. SHE, TOO, WAS A FOUNDLING. AND BEFORE THAT, AN INDIAN.

"TAKE ME HOME, MY LORD." HE DOESN'T REMEMBER, OF COURSE. HE HASN'T WITS ENOUGH.

I WILL HELP. HELP HIM SNATCH FROM MEMORY THE BRIGHT PROMISE OF HIS LIFE; THE GLORIOUS IDEAL; THE TREE; THE LINEAGE.

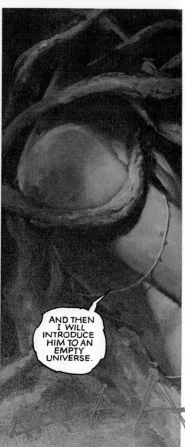

AND THEN I WILL INTRODUCE HIM TO AN EMPTY UNIVERSE.

...I DON'T BELIEVE HE'S GONNA SIT STILL FOR IT MUCH LONGER.

...HE HIRED HIMSELF OUT AS A CARPENTER'S APPRENTICE WITHOUT REALLY KNOWING WHICH END OF THE HAMMER DROVE THE NAIL!

26

SHE SHO' DID. HER LEFT EYE. RIGHT EYE WAS FINE.

SHE HAD A LITTLE MONEY THOUGH, SO SHE GOT HERSELF A GLASS EYE. IT WAS BLUE. DIDN'T MATCH THE RIGHT EYE THOUGH. AND IT WAS TOO SMALL.

HER EYE WAS TOO SMALL?

YESSIR. PERSONALLY I NEVER WANTED TO SIT NEXT TO THAT WOMAN IN CHURCH.

SHE'D GET THE SPIRIT, SHE COME TO GET EXCITED, THAT GLASS EYE WOULD START TO WHIRL AND GO ON WHIRLIN', FLASHIN' FIRST BLUE THEN WHITE, THEN BLUE...

GROWN PEOPLE DIDN'T MIND IT, BUT IT MOST ALWAYS MADE THE CHILDREN CRY.

THE EARTH HAS WAVED ME
INTO THE DARK WATERS
BEYOND LANGUAGE. WORDS
DISAPPEAR INTO THE DEEP
GREEN FORESTS. SEARCHING
THE DARK WITHOUT EYES;
IT IS A THING OF SUBLIME
AND FEARSOME BEAUTY,
LIKE SO MANY SKIES I
HAVE BEEN IN.

I FIND MYSELF MOVING, PLUNGING
THROUGH THE FIRMAMENT. I TASTE
THE SAND AND CLAY OF EACH
COUNTRY AS I MOVE NEARER. I
BREATHE THE COLD STREAMING
SURFACE OF THESE WATERS. I SEND
OUT SIGNALS, QUESTIONS, VIBRATIONS,
INTO THE WORLD AND THE RESPONSES
RETURN, NOT IN A MILLISECOND, BUT
IN THE EXACT SAME MOMENT.

IN THE INFINITE DEPTHS OF THE SKY I FIND THREE STARS.

I FEEL THE ROTATION OF THE EARTH AS I REMEMBER SHE HAS THREE STRAWBERRY MARKS ON HER BACK PLACED JUST LIKE THOSE STARS.

WE WOULD PLAY IN THE YARD AFTER SCHOOL, RAY EDWIN AND I, MAKING UP GAMES OF CHASE AND PAPER AIRPLANES...

...WHENEVER HE WASN'T WORKING, THAT IS. RAY EDWIN HAD BEEN PICKIN' UP THE PECANS FOR TE, MAKING A NICKEL FOR EVERY TREE THEY FINISHED. HE WAS RIGHT PROUD OF HIS JOB...

... AND I WAS MAKING OUT VERY WELL ON THE DEAL; I PROMISED TO KEEP HIS PROFESSION A SECRET FROM MAMA AND IN RETURN, RAY EDWIN WOULD BUY ME A LICORICE TWIST FROM DENNING'S GROCERY.

NEWS OF THE ACCIDENT IN TOWN HAD REACHED US BY WAY OF THE HEDGEROW GOSSIP CHANNELS.

OUR ACTIVITIES HALTED WHEN ANY OF THE NEIGHBORS APPEARED AND WE SILENTLY MADE OUR WAY CLOSE ENOUGH TO HEAR THE GOINGS-ON.

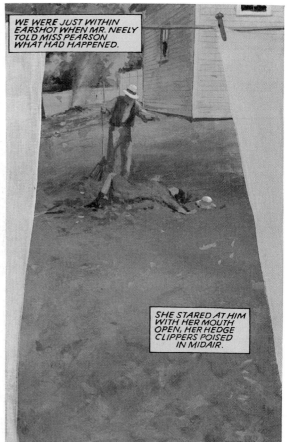

WE WERE JUST WITHIN EARSHOT WHEN MR. NEELY TOLD MISS PEARSON WHAT HAD HAPPENED.

SHE STARED AT HIM WITH HER MOUTH OPEN, HER HEDGE CLIPPERS POISED IN MIDAIR.

THEN SHE TURNED ABOUT THE SAME COLOR AS THE HEDGE AND SLUMPED TO THE GROUND.

I HEARD RAY EDWIN ASK MAMA WHY MISS PEARSON HAD TAKEN THE NEWS ABOUT THE ACCIDENT SO BADLY. AFTER ALL, IT WASN'T AS IF *HER* HUSBAND HAD BEEN RUN OVER. SHE DIDN'T EVEN *HAVE* ONE.

MAMA ANSWERED QUIETLY THAT MISS PEARSON WAS VERY FOND OF THE MEN WHO HAD DIED AND SHE WAS JUST VERY SAD FOR THEIR WIVES AND CHILDREN.

WHEN I OFFERED UP THAT I KNEW MISS PEARSON SURE WAS FOND OF MR. DALTON BECAUSE I HAD SEEN THEM VISITING IN THE CAR MANY TIMES OVER ON THAT SMALL ROAD NEAR THE CORN FIELD, MAMA JUST GAVE ME A LOOK.

RAY EDWIN, TAKE YOUR SISTER INSIDE TO THE CELLAR!

HE STAYED WITH US THROUGH THE NIGHT, WAITING TO BE SURE MAMA WAS ALL RIGHT. SHE WAS A LITTLE SORE BUT NOTHING BROKEN. WHEN THE WIND AND RAIN STOPPED IN THE DAWN HOURS HE SET ABOUT CHOPPING UP THE FALLEN TREE.

I STUDIED TE'S FACE; THIS TALL MAN WITH BEAUTIFUL SKIN, HIS DARK FOREHEAD FURROWED LIKE A NEW-PLOWED FIELD, AS HE WAVED TO ME.

UNDER A CLOUD-CHOKED SKY I SAW HIM IN THE PALE MORNING LIGHT, AND ALSO IN THAT SPECIAL LIGHT, RESERVED BY CHILDREN, FOR THOSE GROWN-UPS WHO LIFT THEM TENDERLY OUT OF A NIGHTMARE AND RESTORE THEIR MORE MANAGEABLE DREAMS.

EVENTUALLY, I CAME TO SEE HOW UNMANAGEABLE THE WORLD COULD BECOME.

MISS PEARSON LINGERED AT HER WINDOW AS TE PASSED. THIS WAS WHERE SHE DID HER BEST WONDERING, PONDERING... SUSPECTING.

THE STORM HAD RIPPED A HOLE IN OUR SLEEPY LITTLE TOWN AND A DARKNESS WAS SNAKING POWERFULLY IN EVERY DIRECTION.

ALL IN ALL WE FARED BETTER THAN MANY.

LIGHTNING HAD STRUCK THE GILLAM BARN. IT WELDED THE DOOR-LATCHES SHUT AND KILLED EVERY ANIMAL INSIDE BUT LEFT THE BUILDING STANDING UNTOUCHED.

THE CLAYBORNS' HANDYMAN SET FIRE TO THEIR GRAINHOUSES CLAIMING THE DEVIL HIMSELF WAS AMONG US.

AND AS IF TO ANNOUNCE THAT ALL THIS TROUBLE WAS UNHOLY WORKINGS, THE WINDS TORE THE CHURCH STEEPLE OFF AND SENT IT A QUARTER MILE AWAY INTO THE AMORYS' CORNFIELD.

AFTER A STORM, THERE ARE USUALLY BIRDS ANNOUNCING THE RETURN OF NORMALCY. THIS MORNING, THERE WERE NO BIRDS.

HEY, BOY.

I SEEN YOU OUT THERE IN POINT TOWNSHIP WITH THAT NIGGER, *BOY*.

DIDN'T YOUR FATHER NEVER TEACH YOU ABOUT NIGGERS?

AW, I FORGOT. YOU AIN'T *GOT* NO FATHER.

MR. OWEN BUTCHIE, SIR?

IS MR. BUTCHIE GONNA COME GIT YOU?

NAAWW,W, HECK. HE'S JUST LETTIN' OFF STEAM. WAY I FIGURE, IF SPITTIN' IN MY FACE AND CALLIN' ME OUT SAVED HIS BOYS ONE EXTRA BEATING, WELL THAT'S SOMETHIN' I RECKON I CAN TAKE.

MR. BUTCHIE IS JUST TRYIN' TO MAKE HIS WAY. HE'S SCARED. HE DON'T HAVE MUCH OPINION OF HISSELF.

43

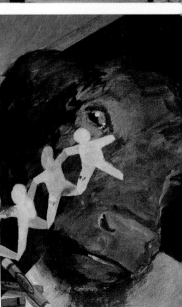

YOU KNOW IT'S THEM BUTCHIES WHAT DONE IT.

I REMEMBER, EVEN NOW, THE WIND WHISPERING IN THE CORNSTALKS WITH A SLIGHT TREMOR SHOOTING UP MY SPINE AS WE WALKED CLOSER TO TE'S HOUSE.

THE SHADOW OF THE TREE ROSE UP, TALL AND DARK, AND FOR ONE RIDICULOUS MOMENT I THOUGHT I SAW AN ENORMOUS SNAKE AT THE BASE OF ITS TRUNK.

IT WAS LOOKING AT ME AND MY FAMILY WITH AN EAGER IMPASSIVITY, A SIMPLE HUNGER.

Mmmm. WE ARE ALMOST ALL HERE NOW.

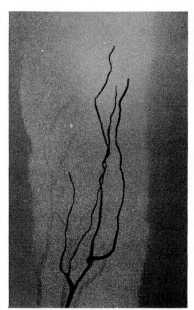

54

I AM NOT A PRISONER.

Mmmm. MY MISTAKE.

BUT, THEN, AREN'T WE *ALL* PRISONERS? YOUR FAMILY, FOR INSTANCE; LITTLE RAY EDWIN.

TRAPPED BECAUSE HIS MEMORY OF YOU IS TAINTED WITH A BLACK SHARD OF VIOLENCE. EVEN NOW, THE EVIL SEED OF WHAT YOU'VE DONE GERMINATES WITHIN HIM.

ONE TINY FIST, CLENCHED IN FEAR, WHICH WILL GROW INTO A GNARLED AND TWISTED HEART. SUCH A GIFT YOU HAVE GIVEN YOUR SON. *ISN'T LIFE WONDERFUL?!*

...LITTLE MAN.

WHY, PAPA? I DIDN'T MEAN TO MAKE YOU MAD.

NO, SON... YOU NEVER...

IT WAS RAINING THAT NIGHT. I HEARD LOUD VOICES AND THE KITCHEN LIGHT WAS ON. I REMEMBERED THAT MAMA WAS WAITING UP WITH SUPPER FOR YOU. SHE WANTED TO TELL YOU ABOUT HER NEW JOB.

I HEARD YOUR VOICE. AT FIRST I COULDN'T SEE ANYTHING BUT SHADOWS.

THEN I SAW MAMA WITH HER ARMS UP IN FRONT OF HER AND THE WAY SHE SHRUNK WHEN THE HAND FLASHED FORWARD. I HEARD THE SICKENING NOISE IT MADE ON HER FACE.

MEG... IT WAS SO HARD. *SHE* COULD FIND WORK. THERE WAS NO WORK.

I COULD SMELL THE WHISKEY ALL THE WAY FROM MY ROOM.

THEN I SAW HER HEAD STRIKE THE KITCHEN WALL. AS SHE SLID TO THE FLOOR, YOU WERE SHOUTING SO LOUD I THOUGHT YOU WOULD BREAK APART.

I JUST WANTED YOU TO STOP! *JUST STOP,* PAPA!

THERE WAS NEVER ENOUGH... MONEY... NEVER ENOUGH TIME.

I WANTED TO BE WITH YOU AND KATIE AND WHEN MEG FOUND WORK, NEITHER OF US WAS GONNA BE WITH YOU...

... IT WAS JUST SO HARD... PLEASE... BELIEVE ME. I NEVER MEANT FOR YOU...

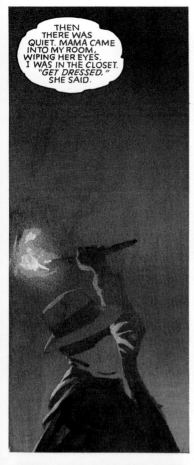

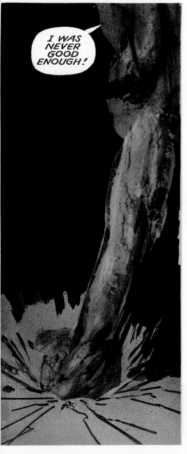

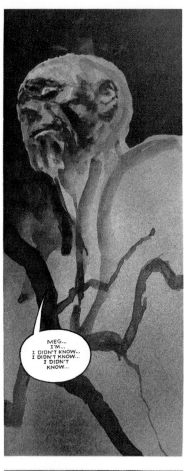

MEG... I'M... I DIDN'T KNOW... I DIDN'T KNOW... I DIDN'T KNOW...

YOU ARE NOT A MAN. *LOOK AT YOU.* YOU ARE A MOCKERY IN A SCARECROW'S CLOTHES.

TRYING DESPERATELY TO BE SOMEONE YOU *THINK* YOU SHOULD HAVE BEEN, SOMEONE WHO NOBODY CARED ABOUT ANYWAY!

THE WORLD IS A WRETCHED PLACE;

FULL OF SUFFERING-- PAIN.

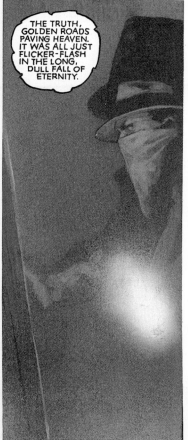

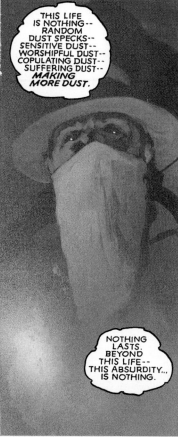

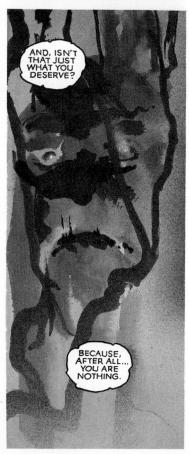

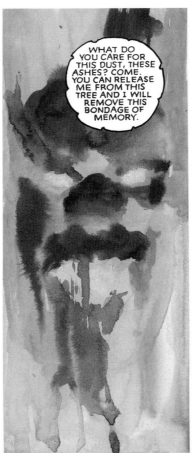

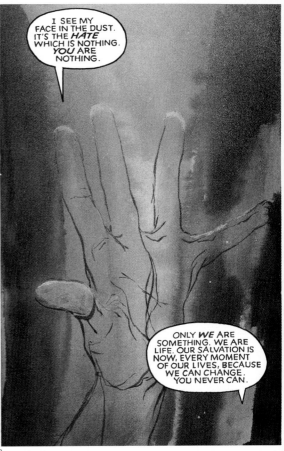

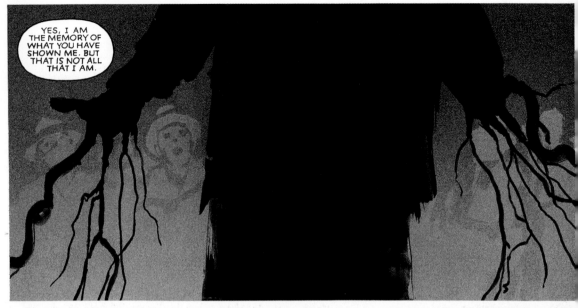

MAMA MADE HER WAY TO TE AND HELD HIM. HE WAS GOING TO BE ALL RIGHT.

AS THEY HAD COME, THE MEN SHUFFLED BACK TO THEIR CARS. DOORS SLAMMED AND ENGINES COUGHED AND THEY WERE GONE. THE GREAT SERPENT HAD UNCOILED ITSELF FROM AROUND THE TREE AND WANDERED AWAY.

I WATCHED THE LEAVES BLOWING AROUND THE DIRT AND THE SCARECROW'S CLOTHES, AND I COULD SMELL THE EARTH. I WAS SUDDENLY PUT IN MIND OF MY FATHER, AND A BEAUTIFUL SPRING DAY WITH A KITE THAT I HAD FORGOTTEN. HE WAS SMILING AND THE SUN TOUCHING HIS FACE MADE HIM HANDSOME. AND I KNEW SOMEHOW I WOULD NEVER FORGET THAT DAY AGAIN.

RAY EDWIN GOT UP AND BROUGHT SOMETHING OVER TO ME, HOLDING IT AS GENTLY AS IF HE WERE CARRYING A ROBIN'S EGG. WHEN HE OPENED HIS HANDS MY MOTHER QUIETLY BEGAN TO CRY. I MARVELED AT THIS BECAUSE SHE CRIED SO SELDOM.

HER HANDS WERE TREMBLING AS SHE SLIPPED IT OVER HER FINGER-- MY FATHER'S WEDDING RING.

TE WAS ALMOST SIXTY-TWO YEARS OLD WHEN THE DEVIL CAME TO POSEY COUNTY. HE ONCE TOLD ME THAT GOOD COMPANY WILL PUT THE BLUES TO FLIGHT.

IN THE WARM BREEZE, I NOTICE A TINY SUGGESTION OF DAWN WAITING UNAFRAID ON THE HORIZON.

THE END